INSPIRED BY
A. A. Milne

Winnie-the-Pooh's
Trivia Quiz Book

DECORATIONS BY
Ernest H. Shepard

Dutton Books
NEW YORK

CIP Data is available.

Published in the United States 1994 by
Dutton Children's Books,
a division of Penguin Books USA Inc.
375 Hudson Street, New York, New York 10014

Written by Joan Powers
Designed by Joseph Rutt

Printed in Hong Kong
10 9 8 7 6 5 4 3 2 1

Winnie-the-Pooh's
Trivia Quiz Book

What name appears over the
doorway of Pooh's house?

Sanders.

What happens to Pooh after eating
a big meal in Rabbit's house?

*He gets stuck trying to leave through
Rabbit's doorway.*

According to Pooh's song, if Bears
were Bees, where would they build
their nests?

At the bottom of trees.

5

When Rabbit asks Pooh whether he wants honey or condensed milk with his bread, what is Pooh's reply?

"Both, but don't bother about the bread, please."

What time does Pooh like a little mouthful of something?

Eleven o'clock in the morning.

Where does Piglet suggest that Pooh dig a Very Deep Pit to catch a Heffalump?

Somewhere where a Heffalump is, just before he falls into it, only about a foot farther on.

Why do Rabbit's friends-and-relations wait hopefully at Pooh's party?

In case anybody speaks to them, or drops anything, or asks them the time.

What is the name of Owl's residence?

The Chestnuts.

How long is Pooh wedged in Rabbit's doorway?

A week.

What kind of book does Christopher Robin read to Pooh when the bear is stuck in Rabbit's doorway?

A Sustaining Book.

What rank of honor does Christopher Robin confer upon Pooh?

Knight.

How does Pooh finally get down
from the sky, when he is floating with
his balloon?

*Christopher Robin shoots the balloon
with his popgun.*

What does Pooh do to try to look
like a small black cloud?

He rolls in the mud.

What is the name of A. A. Milne's
son?

Christopher Robin Milne.

Along with Christopher Robin and Rabbit, who helps pull Pooh out of Rabbit's doorway?

All of Rabbit's friends-and-relations.

Who finds Eeyore's missing tail?

Pooh.

What does Pooh's "sinking feeling" mean?

He's hungry.

What do Pooh and Piglet put in their Heffalump Trap?

A jar of honey.

What does Crustimoney Proseedcake mean?

Customary procedure—the Thing to Do.

What does Pooh sing when he does his Stoutness Exercises in front of the mirror?

Tra-la-la, tra-la-la, Tra-la-la, tra-la—oh, help!—la.

What does Christopher Robin call Piglet when he doesn't recognize him because he is so clean?

Henry Pootel.

What does Pooh sometimes eat for breakfast?

Marmalade spread lightly over a honeycomb or two.

How does Pooh describe his own spelling?

"It's good spelling but it Wobbles, and the letters get in the wrong places."

How does Owl spell his own name?

WOL.

WOL

According to Piglet, what does "TRESPASSERS W" stand for on the sign outside his house?

Trespassers William.

What kind of noise does Piglet make from the bottom of Kanga's pocket?

A squeaky Roo-noise.

How does Piglet try to save himself during the flood?

He sends a message in a bottle.

According to Piglet, what happens when One of the Fiercer Animals is Deprived of Its Young?

It becomes as fierce as Two of the Fiercer Animals.

What was the name of the Milne home in Sussex that inspired the Forest setting of the Pooh stories?

Cotchford Farm.

When Pooh, Christopher Robin,
and the others go on the Expotition,
what are they looking for?

The North Pole.

15

Who is at the end of the line when the Expotition starts?

All of Rabbit's friends-and-relations.

What is Owl's definition of an Ambush?

A sort of Surprise.

How does Tigger move?

He bounces.

What is Roo's Strengthening Medicine made of?

Extract of Malt.

16

How does Pooh find the North Pole?

He picks it up in order to help fish Roo out of the water.

17

What does Pooh like to have at about eleven o'clock in the morning?

A little smackerel of something.

What does Pooh name the spot where he and Piglet build a house for Eeyore?

Pooh Corner.

Where is Small finally located?

On Pooh's back.

18

What is Small's full name?

Very Small Beetle.

How old was James James Morrison
Morrison Weatherby George Dupree?

Three.

What does Alexander Beetle do
when he thinks the entire Expotition
is saying "Hush!" to him?

*He buries himself head downwards in a
crack in the ground, and stays there for two
days, then lives quietly with his Aunt
ever-afterwards.*

What does it mean when Pooh feels a little eleven o'clockish?

He's hungry.

When Pooh and Piglet follow paw-marks in the snow, what do they think might have made the tracks?

Woozles and Wizzles.

What word describes the place where Eeyore lives?

Gloomy.

Who gives an unexpected speech at Pooh's party?

Eeyore.

What is contained in the notice that Rabbit brains out?

"Notice a meeting of everybody will meet at the House at Pooh Corner to pass a Rissolution By Order Keep to the Left Signed Rabbit."

What affectionate expression does Christopher Robin use when he sees that Pooh has gotten himself into trouble?

"Silly old Bear."

What kind of cough does Roo have that prevents him from going on the walk to lose Tigger?

A Biscuit Cough.

Who gets hiccups at Pooh's party?

Roo.

When Pooh wakes up in the morning, what is the first thing he says to himself?

"What's for breakfast?"

What does Eeyore say about Accidents?

"You never have them till you're having them."

What is on the notice that
Christopher Robin pins to his
front door?

GON OUT
BACKSON
BISY
BACKSON.
C. R.

What is the weather like on the
day Rabbit and the others try to lose
Tigger at the top of the Forest?

Cold and misty.

23

What is halfway between Pooh's house and Piglet's house?

A Thoughtful Spot.

What does Pooh sing while he floats in the sky, attempting to get honey from the bees?

How sweet to be a Cloud
Floating in the Blue!
Every little cloud
Always sings aloud.

What does Owl plan to call his new house?

The Wolery.

What does Eeyore think the other animals in the Forest have instead of Brains?

Grey fluff that's blown into their heads by mistake.

Where do the original toys owned by Christopher Robin Milne reside today?

At the Donnell branch of the New York Public Library in New York City.

What does Pooh use to try to get honey? *A balloon.*

Who gets lost in the mist in the attempt to unbounce Tigger? *Rabbit.*

What game do Pooh and the others play at the bridge? *Poohsticks.*

How many verses are in the song Pooh writes in honor of Piglet? *Seven.*

According to the poem, with whom does Christopher Robin go to Buckingham Palace?

Alice.

What does Pooh do with Eeyore's birthday present?

He eats it.

Which of the Pooh characters are based on real toys, and which are not?

Pooh, Kanga, Roo, Piglet, Tigger, and Eeyore are based on real toys; Rabbit and Owl are not.

What hat does Pooh ask Christopher Robin to do to help him steal honey from the bees?

Walk up and down carrying an umbrella, saying, "Tut-tut, it looks like rain."

On whom does Pooh land when he steps on a piece of the Forest left out by mistake?   *Piglet.*

28

Who made the sound
Worraworraworraworraworra outside
Pooh's front door in the middle of
the night? *Tigger.*

In the poem "The King's Breakfast,"
what did the King want for the Royal
slice of bread? *Butter.*

What happens to Owl's house on
the Blusterous day?

It is blown down.

How do Christopher Robin and Pooh rescue Piglet from the flood?

In a boat made from an upside-down umbrella.

What color is the balloon Piglet gives Eeyore for his birthday?

Red.

What do Rabbit, Pooh, and Piglet plan to say once Kanga has discovered that it is Piglet, not Roo, in her pocket?

"Aha!"

What is the Noble Thing that Piglet does for Owl?

He gives him his house.

What words are difficult for Owl to spell?

MEASLES and BUTTERED TOAST.

What does Pooh call his honey-pot
boat?   *The Floating Bear.*

Owl's new house presents one
problem. What is it?
It is already Piglet's house.

In the poem "Vespers," who is saying
his prayers?   *Christopher Robin.*

The pencils in Pooh's Special Pencil
Case are marked "B," "HB," and "BB."
What do these initials stand for?
*"B" is for Bear, "HB" is for Helping Bear,
"BB" is for Brave Bear.*

31

What kind of bush does Pooh land on when he falls from the tree while trying to get honey?

A gorse-bush.

Where did Owl find the bell-rope that Pooh discovers hanging outside Owl's front door?

Hanging over a bush in the Forest.

What do Pooh and Christopher Robin call large grey animals with trunks?

Heffalumps.

Who finds a new house for Owl?

Eeyore.

What kind of sandwiches does Roo like?

Watercress.

What does Eeyore say about birthdays?

Here today and gone tomorrow.

How is Eeyore's tail reattached to his body?

Christopher Robin nails it in place.

Where do Pooh and Piglet get the sticks they use to build a house for Eeyore?

From Eeyore's house on the other side of the wood.

What does Piglet think to himself as he rides in Kanga's pocket?

"If this is flying I shall never really take to it."

Where does Pooh find Eeyore's missing tail?

At Owl's house, where it is being used as a bell-rope.

What does Christopher Robin name the umbrella boat?

The Brain of Pooh.

In the poem "The Four Friends,"
Ernest was an elephant, Leonard was
a lion, and George was a goat.
What was James?

A very small snail.

Which items does Tigger discover
he does not like for breakfast?

Honey, haycorns, and thistles.

What does Kanga give Piglet in
return for his playing a trick on her?

A cold bath and some Strengthening
Medicine.

What does Christopher Robin say
on approaching a Dangerous Place
during the Expotition?

"Hush!"

Why does Pooh need string when
he returns to the Heffalump Trap?

To lead the Heffalumps home.

How do Tigger and Roo get down
from the Pine Tree?

They jump into Christopher Robin's tunic,
which he and the others are holding open.

What does Piglet eat?

Haycorns.

What do Pooh and the others
discover that Christopher Robin does
in the mornings?

He learns. He becomes Educated.

What does Roo call Owl's dirty
sponge?   *A spudge.*

Which animals made the tracks that
Pooh and Piglet follow around the
spinney of larch trees?

Pooh and Piglet.

Who writes a birthday greeting on the honey pot Pooh gives to Eeyore?

Owl.

What happens to the sandwiches Tigger and Roo leave at the bottom of the Pine Tree?

Pooh eats them.

What is the name of the enchanted place at the top of the Forest?

Galleons Lap.

Who winds up in the water during a game of Poohsticks at the bridge?

Eeyore.

What are the names of some of
Rabbit's friends-and-relations?

*Alexander Beetle, Small, Late, Early,
Smallest-of-All, Henry Rush Beetle.*

How does Pooh escape from the
flood?

*He goes to a broad branch of his tree
with ten pots of honey.*

What message does Christopher
Robin tie to the North Pole?

*NORTH POLE
DISCOVERED BY POOH
POOH FOUND IT.*

Why is Piglet wary of Kanga?

*He's afraid a kanga might be One of
the Fiercer Animals.*

What happens to Piglet's present for
Eeyore?

It bursts when Piglet falls on it.

Which of the original toys owned by Christopher Robin Milne has been lost?

Roo, which was lost when the young Milne was still a boy.

How does Pooh get to Christopher Robin's house during the flood?

He floats on a honey pot.

What is printed on the piece of broken board outside Piglet's house?

"TRESPASSERS W."

What things does Kanga like to count when she feels motherly?

Roo's vests, pieces of soap, the two clean spots in Tigger's feeder.

What does Pooh think will happen
if he plants a honeycomb outside
his house?

It will grow up into a beehive.

In the poem "Forgiven," what name
does the boy give his beetle?

Alexander.

What does Eeyore eat?

Thistles.

Why do Pooh and Piglet want to
visit Owl on the Blusterous day?

To have a Proper Tea.

Who takes an unexpected swim during the Expotition to the North Pole?

Roo.

Who is Binker?

An imaginary friend.

What letter does Eeyore form on the ground with sticks?

The letter A.

For whom does Piglet pick a bunch of violets?

Eeyore.

What is a Very Nearly tea?

One you forget about afterwards.

What does Pooh give Eeyore for
his birthday?

A Useful Pot to Keep Things In.

What does Christopher Robin do to
help comfort the Wedged Bear in
Great Tightness?

He reads to him.

43

How do Pooh, Piglet, and Owl
escape from Owl's blown-down
house?

After Piglet is raised to the letter-box on a string, he squeezes out and runs for help.

How does Pooh spell honey?

Hunny.

Which animal, aside from Roo,
takes a ride in Kanga's pocket?

Piglet.

Which of the seven verses that Pooh
wrote about him is Piglet's favorite?

The one that begins "O gallant Piglet."

What does Rabbit do with Pooh's back legs while Pooh is stuck in the doorway?

He hangs his washing on them.

What song does Pooh sing to gloomy Eeyore?

"Cottleston Pie."

What are the names of the two children in the poem "Buttercup Days"?

Anne and Christopher.

What does Piglet wonder when he blows at a dandelion?

Whether it will be this year, next year, sometime or never (but he can't remember what "it" is).

What does Tigger eventually find that he likes to eat?

Extract of Malt.

When Piglet is startled and jumps, how does he try to show he wasn't frightened?

He jumps up and down once or twice in an exercising sort of way.

What does Eeyore say when he looks at himself in the water?

"Pathetic."

When Christopher Robin is a hundred, how old will Pooh be?

Ninety-nine.

What are Provisions?

Things to eat.

What does Pooh know when he sees Christopher Robin putting on his Big Boots?

An Adventure is going to happen.

What does Piglet find when he checks the Heffalump Trap early in the morning?

Pooh with a honey pot stuck on his head.

What does Christopher Robin like doing best? *Nothing.*

Where does Piglet go to live after he gives his own house to Owl? *Pooh's house.*

What gift does Christopher Robin give Pooh at the party? *A Special Pencil Case.*